SCOOBY-DOO!
Mystery #3
The Haunting of Pirate Cove

by
Kate Howard

illustrated by
Duendes del Sur

SCHOLASTIC INC.
New York Toronto London Auckland
Sydney Mexico City New Delhi Hong Kong

ISBN 978-0-545-38678-4

12 11 10 9 8 7 6 5 4 3 12 13 14 15 16 17/0

Designed by Henry Ng

Printed in the U.S.A. 40

First printing, March 2012

CHAPTER 1

"Raggy!" Scooby-Doo poked at his friend.

Shaggy had been dozing in the backseat of the Mystery Machine. He jumped when his pal touched his tummy.

"Hee, hee," Shaggy giggled sleepily. "That

tickles! Stop poking me, sandwich!"

Shaggy wiggled away from Scooby and stretched his arms in the air. Then he opened his eyes and groaned. "Oh, man, Scoob! Like, I was just dreaming about the most perfect sandwich you've ever seen. But you woke me up before I got to take a bite!"

"Rorry," Scooby said. He slowly chewed the last bits of the Scooby Snack he'd sneaked into his mouth while Shaggy was napping. Then he grinned. "Ralmost rere! Rook."

Shaggy rubbed his eyes and peeked out the van window. All he could see was sparkling blue water. It stretched for miles on either side of the van. It almost seemed like the van was driving on top of the water.

"Hey, Fred, old buddy? Like, I think you took a wrong turn somewhere." Shaggy rubbed his eyes again, sure he must be seeing things. "The van seems to have lost the road."

Fred laughed. "We're still on the road, Shaggy. This bridge is just really narrow. It'll take us across the channel between the mainland and the island. The *Ruby Princess* sets sail from an old marina on the island. We'll be there in just a few minutes."

"Yum, yum, yum!" Shaggy cried, rolling down his window. "It smells like ocean out there! And you know what I always say. . . ."

"Rhat?" asked Scooby.

"Like, there's nothing like salty fresh air to build up my appetite!" Scooby cried, patting his belly.

"Ruh-huh!" Scooby agreed, licking his lips hungrily.

"What time did you say this big, fancy meal is happening on the ship tonight?" Shaggy asked Velma.

"The pirate feast is scheduled for sundown," she replied. "*After* we get some exploring in."

Daphne nodded. "That's right. Before we can eat like pirates, we have to survive the high-seas pirate adventure that lies ahead!"

"Rurvive?" Scooby asked nervously.

"Like, I thought you said this ship was safe?" Shaggy said, peering out at the ocean again. Little boats that looked like specks of dust dotted the horizon. The colors of the sky seemed to melt together in bright blue and gold streaks.

"It *is* safe," Fred answered reassuringly. "Daphne is just teasing you. This pirate cruise is going be so much fun. It's the *Ruby Princess*'s maiden voyage, you know! We're among the very first passengers."

The Mystery Inc. gang had been looking forward to a day of boating and swimming for several weeks. They'd been invited to join about forty other people on a replica pirate ship called the *Ruby Princess* for its very first pirate adventure cruise. Guests on the cruise could explore beautiful coral reefs, hidden coves, and even enjoy a high-seas pirate feast.

"Time to slip your eye patch on, old buddy," Shaggy told Scooby as the van bumped off the bridge and onto the sand-covered island drive. He pulled two black eye patches out of his pocket. He and Scooby each slipped a patch over one eye. Then they looked at each other.

"Ahoy there, matey!" Shaggy said, giggling.

"Rahoy!" Scooby growled back.

"Oh, boy," Velma said, rolling her eyes. "This is going to be one long pirate cruise."

Fred eased the van off the road and parked next to a giant sand dune. The gang could see groups of people standing on the other side of the dune. Crowds were gathered around a gangway that led to a looming black and white ship. A pirate flag flew from the mast, and wooden gangplanks stuck out from either side.

"Looks like they're getting the ship ready for our day at sea," Fred observed. The others watched as people dressed like pirates scurried about the deck, pulling at ropes and sails. "I wonder if they could use some help from a knot expert like myself." He stuck out his chest proudly.

"Oh, this is going to be so groovy!" Daphne said, giggling. "I hope we get to dress like pirates, too." She gazed up at the pirates on the ship, who were dressed in pirate hats, scarves, and long, flowing black coats. Daphne looked down at her own dress and frowned. "Or maybe we can just learn some pirate songs. Wouldn't that be fun?"

"Hooks for sale!" A voice rang out behind the gang. "I've got genuine pirate *hooks* for sale!"

A woman selling pirate souvenirs stopped when she noticed Shaggy and Scooby staring greedily at her cart of trinkets. The woman's long brown hair was braided and sticking out from under a bandana. She was wearing a pair of shorts and a loose dark blouse. On her back, she wore

a backpack with THE RUBY PRINCESS stitched on it. Underneath the words there was a picture of a creepy pirate face.

The woman gave them a mean-looking smile, and Shaggy noticed that one of her teeth was covered in gold. "Hello thar," she said. "Would ya like to buy a pirate's hook?"

"Are they really *real*?" Shaggy asked, reaching out to touch one of the hooks. "Like, did you steal them from Captain Hook or something?"

"Reah," Scooby said, giggling. "Raptain Rook!" He grabbed a hook off the pile and held it in his paw. *"Arrr!"* he growled, waving it in the air.

"Ye touch it, ye buy it," the woman said angrily. She squinted at the gang and coughed. Her golden tooth glinted in the sunlight. "Twenty dollars."

"Twenty dollars for a cheap toy hook?" Velma said, frowning. "That's ridiculous."

The woman shrugged. "Too late now. Yer dog took one of me hooks, so ye need to buy it."

Scooby returned to the vendor's cart and dropped the hook back in the box with all the others. "Ro ranks," he muttered sheepishly.

"Fine," the woman spat. "Don't buy it. But I'm the only person that's allowed to sell authentic pirate hooks around here. Good ol' Sally's got an exclusive arrangement with the ship, y'know." She grinned evilly. "And yer gonna be sorry later, when ya *wish* you had a hook!"

"Why would we be sorry?" Daphne asked.

The woman leaned in and whispered, "Because the real pirates in these parts are always watchin' ya, ready to pounce. And y'never know when yer gonna need something to fight 'em off!" She tipped back her head and laughed.

"Real pirates?" Shaggy asked nervously. "Like, *what* real pirates?" He gulped.

The woman chuckled. "Tell the ghosts of long-ago pirates out at sea that Sassy Sally says hello!" Then she stalked away.

Shaggy and Scooby stared after her. They looked scared.

Suddenly, Sassy Sally turned and called out over her shoulder, "I'm just tellin' stories."

Shaggy and Scooby both let out a sigh of relief.

But they sucked that sigh right back in again when the woman flashed her creepy smile at them one last time. "Unless they're *not* stories . . . wait till ye see what's out thar in the ocean deep. Maybe ya want to think about staying on dry land, eh?"

She laughed and disappeared into the crowd.

CHAPTER

2

"I think that golden-toothed hook lady is on to something," Shaggy observed. He watched as Sassy Sally stopped and offered to sell hooks and swords to some of the ship's other passengers. "Like, I've got a good idea, guys. How about we just get some chairs and a few fishing poles? We can spend the afternoon right here on the dock."

He looked around hopefully. Scooby was nodding eagerly.

Shaggy turned to Velma, Fred, and Daphne. "What do you say? Like, I noticed a restaurant just over there, and there's a cart that has fudge and saltwater taffy for sale."

But Fred, Velma, and Daphne were shaking their heads.

"Maybe we can catch some fish, do a little swimming," Shaggy suggested. He pinched his nose closed and pretended to jump from the dock into the water.

"You don't need to worry, Shaggy," Fred said, trying to reassure him. "You heard that woman say she was just fooling with you. The ship's crew are all just acting—it's their job to try to make us think we're in some kind of danger. That's what makes a pirate adventure cruise fun!" Fred put his hands on his hips and looked out to sea. "We're going to have a great time on the boat. Fishing, scuba diving, exploring—you're going to love it."

Daphne patted Shaggy on the shoulder. "And don't forget about the pirate feast after the day's adventures."

"Sure," Shaggy muttered. "They're probably planning to feast on *us*. Ha, ha, the joke's on us. Like, once we all get on board, I bet they're planning to tie us up and take us prisoner. And then it's going to be Shaggy on a stick for the feast tonight!"

Velma laughed. "Oh, stop being such a chicken, Shaggy. It's not like we're headed out to sea with *real* pirates. All of this is made up. Like Fred said, they're *actors*."

Fred, Velma, and Daphne continued exploring the marina, but neither Shaggy nor Scooby were enjoying themselves anymore. They were nervous about what Sassy Sally had said. As the two buddies wandered along the dock, they kept peering anxiously over their shoulders.

"If we really have to go out on this boat, then can someone loan me twenty dollars?" Shaggy said as they passed a dockhand with a large sword tied to his rope belt. "Like, Scooby and I both think it would be a good idea to buy one of those hooks. Or maybe a sword?"

"We're not buying a hook from a woman selling toys on the dock," Velma said, shaking her head. "Shaggy, we went over this. There's no such thing as pirates around here, and the people who work for the *Ruby Princess* are just goofing around. People are going to try to scare you all day—that's the whole point of an authentic pirate cruise."

"Velma's right," Daphne said. "It wouldn't be as much fun if they didn't try to make you think you were part of the action. Just pretend you're one of the shipmates, and let's have some fun, guys!"

Scooby whispered something to Shaggy, and Shaggy nodded. Then he said, "Scoob and I will feel better prepared for the *action* if we have a hook to protect ourselves. So, who's going to buy one for us?"

"A hook, eh?" A man dressed in pirate garb suddenly popped out from behind one of the wooden pilings on the dock. He had a dark, purplish-black beard and was wearing a hook as a hand. He waved it at them. "A hook like this?"

Fred jumped, startled. *"Yikes!"* When he realized it was just another dockhand in costume, he nervously adjusted his ascot. "Well, hey there, friend," he said, trying to laugh it off. "You surprised me!"

"Surprised ya?" the dockhand grumbled. "Thar be a lot of surprises in store for ya today." The man's voice was low and rumbling, and the look on his face wasn't very friendly. His purple beard had been twisted into knots that looked like they'd be hot in the summer sun. He held the same *Ruby Princess* backpack as Sassy Sally. "Are ye ready for adventure?"

"You bet we are," Fred said loudly. He stood with his hands on his hips, acting bold. "Ahoy!" It was clear he was embarrassed that a pretend pirate with a fake hook had frightened him just a few seconds before. "I'm Fred. This is Daphne, Velma, Shaggy, and Scooby-Doo . . . five adventurers, reporting for our pirate cruise!" He saluted.

"Ahoy yerself," the man in black said. He gave Fred a funny look, then turned to the others. "I'm Purple Beard, a deckhand and the ship's cook."

"The ship's cook, huh?" Shaggy asked. "Can you tell me if I look . . . um . . . *delicious* to you?"

Just then, a gong rang out. That was the signal that it was time for the *Ruby Princess* to set sail. Everyone on the dock swarmed toward the boat.

The deckhand glanced up. "Time to pop on board," he said. "I jest hope we all make it back from our maiden voyage."

Fred, Daphne, and Velma laughed. Purple Beard looked at them like they were crazy, and then tugged at his beard.

"Don't know why yer laughing, since I'm not foolin'," Purple Beard said. "Y'know where we're goin', right?" He strode alongside the gang as they made their way toward the ship. "This cruise is headed for Pirate Cove. The captain decided to set up an authentic treasure hunt on the land around Pirate Cove. None of us deckhands are sure why he decided to do it there."

"What's the matter with Pirate Cove?" Velma wondered.

"Don't ya know?" Purple Beard said menacingly. "Pirate Cove is haunted."

Shaggy and Scooby stopped in their tracks, but Velma pulled them along. She was sure Purple Beard was just telling stories to try to scare them.

Purple Beard continued, "Pirate Cove is haunted by the ghosts of angry pirates. Some people think it's just silly stories meant to frighten children, but people who have lived around these parts for a while know that the legend is true."

"Rue?" Scooby asked.

"Like, you mean pirates live here?" Shaggy whispered.

"Not here, exactly," Purple Beard said with a smile. "But on the island where we're going,

Pirate's Cove? Yep, thar be pirates."

"Real, rive rirates?" Scooby asked, tucking his head under Shaggy's arm.

"Real pirates, yes," Purple Beard answered. "But *alive*? No siree. The cove is haunted by the ghosts of pirates long departed. They hang around to protect the treasure that's said to be hidden on the island. Anyone who comes near—snap! They take 'em prisoner."

"Ha!" Fred said. "You're just telling stories to try to make us nervous. For fun, right?"

"It's all fun and games, until someone gets hurt," Purple Beard said, scratching at the skin under his beard with the hook at the end of his hand. "If I were ye, I wouldn't search for treasure in Pirate Cove unless yer looking for trouble."

With that, Purple Beard grabbed a rope hanging from the side of the ship and climbed up to the main deck. He vaulted over the deck rail and strode off toward the rear of the ship. "Remember!" he called out one last time. "Stay away from Pirate Cove!"

CHAPTER 3

"Welcome aboard!" a booming voice cried as Shaggy, Scooby, Velma, Fred, and Daphne walked up the gangway to the ship's main deck. "Ahoy, mateys!"

"Ahoy!" Fred called out in response.

"Are ye ready for the maiden voyage of the *Ruby Princess*?" the man asked, winking. At least, it looked like it was supposed to be a wink. But it was more like a blink, since one of his eyes was hidden under an eye patch.

The one-eyed man leaned toward them. His big belly jiggled under his pirate outfit. His head was covered in a kerchief, and tufts of black hair stuck out at odd angles around his neck. "I'll be yer captain today. Call me Captain Johnny. We'll take excellent care of ya . . . unless there's trouble, that is. If we run into trouble, then it's every man, woman—and dog!—for himself."

Captain Johnny chuckled, but Shaggy didn't think his joke was very funny. He turned and walked back toward the dock. "Like, that's it, I'm outta here," he announced.

"Re, roo," said Scooby, following his friend.

"Where are ya headed off to?" Captain Johnny called after Shaggy. "The pirate adventure cruise is back this way, y'know. Ye have to board the ship if ye want to sail the high seas with Johnny and his crew."

"Shaggy," Velma called. "Come back on the boat. You know that Purple Beard and Sassy Sally were just fooling with you. You're not in any danger on the pirate cruise! Stop being such a scaredy-cat."

"Danger?" Captain Johnny asked with a grin. "Of course there's no real danger. Me deckhands are just having a bit of fun, that's all."

"See?" said Velma.

Shaggy turned back and looked up at Captain Johnny. "So you're saying there *aren't*, like, ghosts of pirates out at Pirate Cove?"

The captain laughed heartily. "Ghosts? Wouldn't that be fun?" When he saw that Shaggy and Scooby didn't think that would be fun at all, he added, "Of course not!"

"No ghosts?" Shaggy asked again, creeping closer to the ship.

"No ghosts," Captain Johnny said with a nod.

The gong sounded again, and Fred noticed that deckhands had begun untying the ropes that held the boat to the dock.

"Now get on board, or yer gonna be left behind, matey!" Captain Johnny adjusted his eye patch and grinned again. "On second thought, maybe ya *should* stay back. Then *I* can eat yer food at the feast tonight!"

At the mention of the pirate feast, Shaggy hustled back up the gangplank. "The feast! Like, you don't have to tell me twice!" The pirate ghosts were quickly forgotten.

Shaggy trailed behind the Captain as he made his way up to the ship's wheel. "I have an important question before the boat sets sail. Captain Johnny, do you happen to know what kind of food they'll be serving at the feast?"

Captain Johnny licked his lips. "Oh, I sure do. I don't want to ruin all the surprises, but I will tell ya that Purple Beard's cheese biscuits have caused more than a few fights among the crew. He's quite a cook, even with a hook for one hand, so I hope yer gonna be hungry!"

"Oh, no need to worry about that," Velma muttered. "Shaggy is *always* hungry."

"Speaking of which," Shaggy said. "Any chance the kitchen needs some help? Maybe Scooby and I could take a peek and see what they're up to. We're excellent chefs."

"I'll leave that up to ya," Captain Johnny said, laughing. "Sassy Sally's down in the galley, too, but they do sometimes need an extra hand."

"Rassy Rally?" Scooby groaned. "Ruh-roh!"

"Now, mateys, I'm afraid I have to say farewell," Captain Johnny said. "I've got a boat to captain and a crew to control. I hope ya all enjoy yerselves. Our next stop is Pirate Cove. We'll stop in an hour or so for swimming, clamming, and the treasure hunt."

Captain Johnny strode off. Moments later, a giant bell rang, and the *Ruby Princess* pulled away from the dock.

"Adventure, here we come!" cried Fred.

CHAPTER 4

Scooby, Shaggy, and the gang spent the next hour wandering around the ship, poking into all its nooks and crannies. They didn't find the kitchen, but they did find a room filled with fake pirate treasures and another room that would obviously serve as the dining room later in the afternoon.

After a bit of exploring, Daphne came upon some empty lounge chairs on the outside deck. She and Scooby sat down to relax and get some sun while the boat chugged its way out to sea.

Meanwhile, Shaggy went in search of snacks. He found a little concessions stand on the lower deck and ordered strawberry lemonades for himself, Scooby, and Daphne. He also filled a tray with snacks, but most of the treats were in his belly before he made it back to his friends. He offered Scooby and Daphne a small handful of wrapped sweets and a sandwich to share.

Scooby quickly gobbled up his portion of sandwich, and then ate Daphne's, too. Just as he was about to swallow the sweets, Daphne grabbed them and stuffed them into her pocket. "I'm going to save some treats for later," she said. "I know you guys are going to be hungry when we get to Pirate Cove, and this way I'll have a few special snacks hidden in my pocket for you when you do!"

Shaggy and Scooby grumbled. But they knew Daphne had their best interests at heart. When it came to snacks, she always kept them in good supply.

As the boat sailed along, Fred strolled around

the deck, chatting with the other passengers. He kept an eye on the deckhands as they tied knots and tugged at ropes and pulleys. He got lessons in granny knots and square knots and something called the Fisherman's Bend.

A deckhand also taught him a special knot that only the crew of the *Ruby Princess* used. It was called the Ruby Rope. When Fred found the others, he gave them all lessons in knot-tying, too. Shaggy paid attention for a few minutes, but after Fred finished with the Ruby Rope, Shaggy got a little sleepy. He yawned and slipped back into his dream about sandwiches.

Sails were raised and lowered, and through it all the deckhands sang pirate songs and put on little shows for the passengers. The crew would pretend to get in brawls, then fight and argue loudly. Usually, the pretend fight would end with someone falling from a high-up platform or swinging dangerously from a rope. But eventually, the crew member would land safe on the deck again. This made everyone laugh and cheer.

Velma went to watch Captain Johnny in action. He gave her a lesson in what all the different dials in the captain's wheelhouse meant. Captain Johnny even let Velma steer the boat for a while.

Everyone was having a great time. After his nap, Shaggy had all but forgotten the warnings about ghosts of pirates at Pirate Cove. He had a full belly and was relaxed and happy.

After sailing for an hour or more, the boat slowed and several of the deckhands lowered the ship's anchor.

"Land ahoy!" someone yelled from up in the crow's nest. "Thar be Pirate Cove!"

All the ship's passengers ran toward the rails that lined the decks. Everyone peered toward land, admiring a beautiful, protected cove that was surrounded on all sides by lush, dense forest. Pirate Cove was sandy and smooth, and gentle waves licked at the shore.

"Everyone line up!" Captain Johnny called from the upper deck. "We'll be taking everyone ashore in groups on the life boats. Me mighty crew will row ye to shore, landlubbers!"

The pirate crew grumbled, pretending to be angry about having to row people to shore. But as everyone piled into boats, it was clear that they didn't mind.

As the gang boarded one of the lifeboats, Shaggy thought he noticed Sassy Sally among the passengers riding toward shore. But when he looked again, she was gone.

Scooby and the gang settled into a lifeboat with Purple Beard, Captain Johnny, and a few other crew members and passengers. As Purple

Beard and another deckhand rowed them toward shore, the pirates all sang songs about forgotten treasure and danger on the sea.

One of the other passengers on the boat struck up a conversation with Fred and Daphne as they bobbed through the water toward Pirate Cove.

"So, are you here for treasure?" the man snapped. "I'll find it before you." He narrowed his eyes at Fred, then studied Daphne, Velma, Shaggy, and Scooby warily.

"Oh, Kurt, hush," the man's wife said, swatting the man on the back of his hand. "Stop talking about treasure. It's all pretend. You don't have to act like this is a competition."

"I won't hush," Kurt announced. "I'm here for

real treasure, and I intend to find it." He spoke loudly enough that several members of the crew stopped singing and turned to look at him. But Purple Beard and Captain Johnny continued to sing and clap merrily as they rowed toward shore.

"Do you mean the treasure hunt Captain Johnny is setting up for the passengers of the *Ruby Princess*?" Velma asked.

"No, I do not," Kurt said, gritting his teeth. "I'm talking about the *real* treasure. The real pirate treasure they say is buried somewhere out here near Pirate Cove."

Captain Johnny was still singing, but everyone else was listening to Kurt now.

"Real treasure?" Fred wondered aloud. "I thought this was all just a game? Isn't Captain Johnny in charge of everything?"

"They're saying this is all just for fun, part of the cruise," Kurt said, more quietly this time. He seemed to have realized that others were listening. "But I'm telling you, there's real treasure buried out here. The first person to find it will be rich!"

"Kurt!" the man's wife scolded. "Stop talking about it!" She pursed her lips.

"You're right, Barb," Kurt nodded. "I shouldn't tell anyone about it. In fact, I should be keeping my mouth closed. I don't need anyone else looking for my pirate's booty." Kurt made a big show of zipping his mouth closed. His wife rolled her eyes.

But it seemed like Kurt couldn't keep his promise. After a few minutes, he was at it again. "Maybe there is no pirate treasure," he muttered. "But if there is, coming on this cruise is the only way I could look for it."

"If you're convinced there is treasure out here, I don't understand why you would wait until all these people are around to look for it," Velma pointed out.

Kurt nodded. "Yes, you make a good point. But the thing is, they say ghosts of pirates haunt Pirate Cove. People who know this area—some of the deckhands themselves, even—have told me that the pirates have kidnapped everyone who's ever tried to hunt for their treasure! But today, there are enough people around to distract the pirate ghosts, so I can search for their treasure in peace."

"Kurt! Hush!" Barb gave her husband an exasperated look. She poked through the backpack on her lap.

Shaggy noticed she had a hook inside her pack. It was just like the ones Sassy Sally had been selling. It was hidden deep inside her backpack, which had the same creepy pirate face as the ones the souvenir seller and Purple Beard had been wearing.

"Hey, where'd everyone get that backpack? I want one." Shaggy pointed to the inside of Barb's pack and asked, "Can I try out your hook?"

Barb looked up, startled. Then she said, "I don't know what you're talking about. I don't have a hook."

As she zipped her backpack closed, the pirates pulled their boat up onto the shore. Everyone stepped out onto the sand.

But they all stopped in their tracks when they saw a handwritten sign posted in the middle of the beach: STAY AWAY OR ELSE!

CHAPTER 5

"Rikes!" Scooby barked. He leaped back into the lifeboat. "Ret's ro!"

"Scoob's right," Shaggy said. He turned around and ran into the shallow waves licking the shore. "Like, let's get out of here!"

"Ha, ha!" Captain Johnny was standing on shore, staring at the sign stuck in the sand.

He laughed mightily when he read it. "I see some of me crew are trying to spook the land-lubbers. Guess we better keep our eye out for pirates!"

"Rook rus?" Scooby said, confused.

"Well, it worked," Shaggy said. "I have an idea! Like, how about we all head back to the *Ruby Princess* and start the pirate feast a little early? Who's with me?"

"Sounds mighty fine to me!" Purple Beard said. "Everyone to the ship!"

"I'm not leaving this island until we do the treasure hunt," Kurt announced sullenly. He stood next to Barb, who had set her backpack down on the edge of the beach.

"Come on, guys," Fred said to Scooby and Shaggy. "It's all just part of the game. The sign isn't real. . . . You guys sure are spooked today! Stop taking everything so seriously."

Captain Johnny nodded. "He's absolutely right. Purple Beard, we'll eat later. All these rumors about the ghosts of pirates haunting Pirate Cove are fun! I've heard me crew telling those stories, but it's all just hearsay." He stomped his foot, and his belly jiggled under his shirt. "Now, give me a few minutes to get the treasure hidden. Then I'll give everyone a copy of the map and send you off in search of the mighty pirate treasure!"

Everyone relaxed on the beach while Captain Johnny headed off into the woods. He was carrying a big sack that hid his treasure chest from view.

All the passengers were enjoying themselves, except for Scooby and Shaggy. They watched the edge of the beach carefully, waiting for the captain to reemerge from the thick brush.

"What if he gets taken prisoner while he's out there?" Shaggy whispered to Scooby.

"Ro risoners," Scooby whined.

"Like, I don't know how to drive a pirate ship. Do you?"

Scooby shook his head.

Shaggy thought for a moment. "Well, I guess we could learn."

After fifteen minutes or so, the captain emerged from the woods. "All right, me hearties, let the treasure hunt begin!"

Some of the ship's passengers gathered around and took a map from Captain Johnny. Others preferred to relax on the beach and soak up the sun.

Most of the ship's crew had returned to the ship to prepare for the pirate feast. Several of the deckhands had ventured into the woods surrounding Pirate Cove. They were ready to help passengers who got lost or needed a hint while they were searching for Captain Johnny's hidden treasure.

As the passengers studied the map, Johnny explained the rules of the treasure hunt. It was an old-fashioned map with strange markings and a big, red *X* in the middle.

Captain Johnny hollered out, "The only rule is: There are no rules! First one to figure out me map and find their way through to the treasure chest wins. Whoever returns to the beach with the prize will be me special guest at the Captain's Table for the pirate feast tonight! That means extra dessert, all-ye-can-eat food, and a meal you'll remember for a long time. Now, good luck, and may the best treasure hunter win!"

"Did you hear that, Scoob?" Shaggy whispered. "We could be Captain Johnny's guests at the feast tonight!"

"Reah," Scooby barked. "Rummy!"

"Should we stick together to search for treasure, or do you want to split up?" Velma asked.

"If we split up, there's a better chance that one of us will find Johnny's treasure—we can look more places," Fred reasoned.

"I'll go with Shaggy and Scooby," Velma offered. "Fred, you and Daphne can hunt together. Just yell if you find anything."

"Sounds good," Fred agreed. "Ahoy!"

"Ahoy," Velma muttered. She was already busy checking out the map. Shaggy and Scooby peered over her shoulder.

"Come on, guys, I think I know where to start," Velma declared. She led Scooby and Shaggy into the woods.

The brush was thick, and the heat hung heavy inside the dense canopy of trees. "Like, I could go for some more of that strawberry lemonade," Shaggy said, panting. "All this treasure hunting sure is making me hungry!"

"We've been in the woods for three minutes, Shaggy," Velma told him. "That's hardly enough time to work up an appetite." She stopped to study the map. "According to this, it looks like there's a hill up ahead. If we cross over the top of that, we should come to a rock that's shaped like a heart. . . ."

Velma broke off suddenly as the sound of someone screaming came from the woods off to their left. "Velma! Fred! Help!"

"Jinkies!" Velma cried. "That's Daphne!" She plunged deeper into the woods. Shaggy and Scooby ran after her.

A huge, looming tree stood in front of them. Fred was standing under it, looking up into its branches.

"Fred! What happened?" Velma called. "Where's Daphne?"

"I don't know," Fred said, looking worried. "We were together one minute, and then I stopped to admire a rope trap that was strung between two branches. When I looked up, Daphne was gone. I heard her yelling for help a moment later."

"She's missing?" Shaggy gulped.

"I wonder where she could be?" Fred wondered. He put his hand over his eyes as a sun-shield and scanned the lush forest.

"Wherever she went, she didn't go by choice," Velma said. "Look at this!"

The others gathered around. They gasped when they saw what Velma was pointing to. A sharp pirate hook was hanging from a nearby tree. A piece of paper was stuck under its point.

Fred walked over and unpinned it. It read, *LEAVE NOW, OR YER FRIEND STAYS WITH US . . . FOREVER!*

CHAPTER 6

"Purple Beard was telling the truth!" Shaggy said. "Maybe Pirate Cove *is* haunted by ghosts of pirates. They didn't like us poking around on their turf, so now they've taken

Daphne as their prisoner. Like, how else can you explain what happened?"

"Look at this!" Velma called from a few steps away. "It's a backpack." She pointed to a backpack that lay at the base of a tree. Some of its contents were strewn on the ground. There was an old white shirt, some rope, and a pirate hat on the ground. "Maybe this is a clue that will help us find Daphne."

"I've seen that backpack before," Fred said.

"It's just like the backpack that Kurt's wife, Barb, was wearing!" Velma exclaimed.

"Sassy Sally had the same one," Shaggy added.

"Rand Rurple Reard," Scooby said.

Fred nodded. "This is a great clue." He scanned the woods, looking for signs of Daphne. "Gang, I think we've got a mystery on our hands."

"A mystery?" A voice rang out behind them, and the gang all turned to see Barb and Kurt hurrying toward them. "What kind of mystery? Did you find the treasure?" Kurt was obviously worried that someone had found the real pirate treasure before he could.

"No, we didn't find real pirate treasure," Velma said. She studied the area around them for footprints or other marks. "We think Daphne's been taken prisoner. Did you see her? Or notice anything suspicious?"

Kurt shook his head, but he didn't look surprised. "No, we didn't see her. I told you there were ghosts on this island. I warned all you kids, but no one ever listens to me."

"Why would anyone listen to you?" Barb asked grouchily. "All you talk about is treasure, treasure, treasure."

"What if one of *us* gets taken prisoner next?" Kurt wondered aloud, suddenly looking nervous. "Maybe we should get back to the mainland and just forget about this whole treasure-hunting business."

Velma frowned. "We can't leave Pirate Cove! We need to find Daphne. She's out here somewhere. Plus, I have a feeling we're not looking for a *ghost*, but an actual *person* who's trying to scare us all away."

"It worked. I'm scared," Kurt said. "Obviously someone's trying to scare us into leaving well enough alone. I think we should just leave your friend behind and save ourselves."

"Kurt!" Barb yelped. "That's a horrible thing to suggest."

"Well, you all can do whatever you want, but I'm headed back to shore. I don't care about finding the treasure. I'm getting out of these woods and away from Pirate Cove," Kurt huffed. "I'm certainly not going to just stand here, waiting for whoever it is to snatch me up, too! If I were you, I'd do the same."

Kurt stomped off in the direction of the beach.

Barb sighed. "Sorry about him," she said. "He's all worked up about this treasure hunt." She hurried after her husband. As she crept under a low-hanging tree, her backpack caught on a branch. Barb yelped in surprise.

Fred and Velma exchanged looks. "Are you thinking what I'm thinking?" Fred asked.

"I think so," Velma said with a nod. "Those two sure are acting strange—and they really want to keep other people from finding that treasure. I wonder if they had anything to do with Daphne's disappearance."

"Well, if they were involved, they're not with her now," Fred replied. "Let's hunt for clues and see if we can find anything else that will help lead us to Daphne."

Velma stooped down to inspect the backpack on the ground more closely. "Look!" she cried, unzipping the pack the rest of the way. "This backpack is stuffed with pirate hooks." She pulled one of the hooks out of the backpack and held it up for the others to see.

"Those are just like the ones that Sassy Sally

was selling on her souvenir cart," Fred observed. "Do you think she has anything to do with this?"

"Like, I thought I saw her getting into one of the little boats when we got to Pirate Cove," Shaggy said. "Maybe she followed us out here to scare everyone away?"

"So, it's possible she is involved," Velma said thoughtfully.

The four friends walked a little further through the forest, searching for more clues.

"Fred, did you say you saw a rope trap hanging in the trees?" Velma asked.

"That's right," Fred said. "Do you think that has something to do with this?"

"We won't know unless we take a closer look," Velma said. "Can you find it again?"

"I think so," Fred said. "Follow me, Velma. Shaggy, Scooby, you two stay here in case Daphne comes back."

"Rokay," Scooby said.

As Fred and Velma began to scan the area, Shaggy glanced at Scooby. "Sure," he muttered. "We'll just sit here, waiting to see if the pirate ghost comes back to find us. . . ."

The two buddies looked around nervously. They could hear the hooting of birds and the chirping of insects in the trees around them.

"Like, no worries, Scoob," said Shaggy. "These

are all just normal sounds of nature. And what could be better than nature? Right?"

"Reah, right," said Scooby, nodding.

Just then, they heard a loud snap. It sounded like a branch crunching under someone's foot.

"Maybe that's Daphne!" Shaggy said hopefully. "I bet she has snacks for us."

But it wasn't Daphne. A low, rumbling voice growled, "*Arrr!* I took yer friend, and you'll be next if ye don't get off me island!"

Shaggy gulped. He looked around, but there was no one behind them. Then he looked up. Dangling in the air above them was a pirate's hook. The hook was attached to the ghostly form of a pirate hidden behind a clump of tree branches. The pirate's jacket was worn and frayed and washed out. It looked ancient. It was hard to see the pirate's face because it was hidden beneath the brim of a big pirate cap.

That was okay with Shaggy. He really didn't want to look any closer. He was frozen with fear.

"Like, Scoob?" he said.

"Reah?" Scooby was looking up at the hook hanging above them. He was shaking from the tips of his ears to the top of his tail. Despite the heat, his teeth were chattering.

"Are you thinking what I'm thinking?"

Scooby nodded eagerly. "Ret's run!"

CHAPTER 7

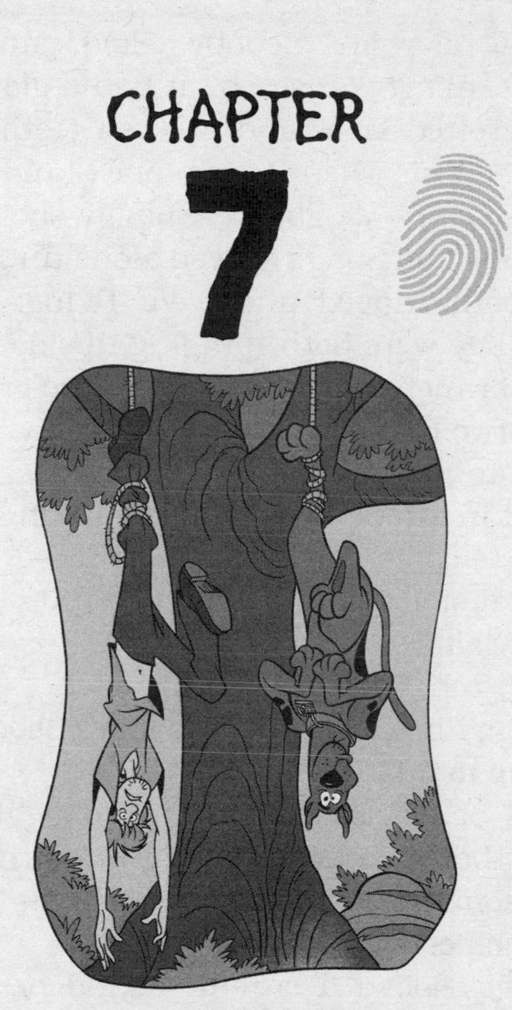

Scooby and Shaggy sped through the forest. They were going so fast, they didn't even look behind them to see if the ghost pirate was following them. But they could hear his laughter echoing through the trees.

“Rhat ras rhat?” Scooby asked, panting.

“Like, didn’t you see it? It had a glowing hook, and a rotted arm, and pointed teeth. I know a pirate ghost when I see one—and that was *definitely* a pirate ghost!” Shaggy shouted.

Scooby and Shaggy raced along until suddenly, they both tripped and went flying. A moment later, they were both hanging upside down from a tree branch about five feet off the ground.

The two friends squirmed and shook their feet, trying to get free, but it was no use. They were caught in a rope trap. Had the pirate ghost been trying to catch them, too?

“Zoinks! I think we found Fred’s rope trap,” Shaggy said.

“Ruh-roh,” sighed Scooby.

Shaggy began to giggle. “Like, Scoob, are you tickling me?”

“Ro,” Scooby said. He began to giggle, too.

But they stopped laughing when they realized that someone—or some*thing*—was poking at their bellies with a hook.

Shaggy jolted to attention and began to pull at the ropes that tied them up. “Like, it’s a good thing I was listening when Fred gave us that lesson in knots this morning!”

A moment later, Shaggy had them both untied. He and Scooby tumbled to the ground. They immediately leaped to their feet and started off through the trees again. The pirate growled and huffed behind them.

Shaggy and Scooby fled all the way back to the beach, where they found some of the *Ruby Princess*'s other passengers lounging in the sun. No one there seemed to realize that anything was amiss.

Kurt and Barb were nowhere to be seen. Neither were Fred or Velma.

Shaggy looked around, desperate to find someone to help them. He spotted the *Ruby Princess*'s captain and ran over.

"Captain Johnny!" he cried. "Captain Johnny! It's real! There's really a pirate ghost in the woods."

Captain Johnny stepped toward Scooby and

Shaggy. "That's impossible," he said. "Why would ye think that?"

"It took Daphne! And then we saw it, hanging in midair in the forest. And it poked us!"

"Reah, roked!" Scooby said, nodding eagerly. "Re raw rit! *Rarrr!*"

"Like, it was chasing us and trying to take us prisoner, too, but we got away just in time," Shaggy explained.

Just then, Fred and Velma dashed out of the woods. Scooby and Shaggy could see the bushes rustling in the woods right behind them. Whatever had been chasing them stopped just before it reached the beach.

A figure in a long black pirate's coat shook its hooked arm from behind the tree line, and then disappeared back into the thick brush.

There was a moment of shocked silence as the passengers on the beach stared after the pirate ghost. Then everyone screamed and began to run for the boats.

"We've got to get out of here!" someone shouted.

"Everyone, to the ship!" another passenger yelled.

"Wait a minute!" Velma said loudly. "Let's all just calm down."

That stopped the passengers. They gathered around her.

"Pirate Cove isn't haunted," Velma explained. "Not by a real ghost, anyway. Unless pirate ghosts carry fake hooks and wear backpacks."

"How can ye be sure?" Captain Johnny said.

"Let's just say that mysteries are our specialty," Velma explained with a smile. "And I've got a pretty good idea of who our 'ghost' really is."

Fred nodded. "The question is why this person is trying to scare us all away. And more importantly . . . what have they done with Daphne?" He put one hand on his hip. "I think it's time for us to set a trap of our own. Let's take the ghost of Pirate Cove prisoner, and make our hooked friend give us some answers!"

"Whoever's behind this better be ready to tell me why he's ruining me cruise," Captain Johnny said with a growl. "Or I'll make 'im walk the plank!"

CHAPTER 8

Fred explained his plan to everyone. "Here's how this will work. Velma and I are going to set a trap—"

Shaggy cut him off before he could continue. "Let me guess. Me and Scoob are the bait, right?"

"Roh, no," Scooby said, shaking his head.

"Oh, yes, Scooby," said Velma. "That's the only way this will work!"

Fred nodded. "You two will pretend you've found the *real* treasure. You'll sit under a tree holding Captain Johnny's treasure chest, which is filled with fake jewels. When our pirate ghost realizes you have what it's been looking for, it'll come running. Velma and I will be standing nearby with a rope trap to catch our hooked crook."

"Easy, right?" Velma said.

"Like, I'm with Scoob," Shaggy said. "There's no way you're getting me back into that jungle again. Can't someone else be pirate bait?"

"Don't you guys want to find Daphne?" Velma scolded.

"Um, yes?" Shaggy said. "But there must be some other way to lure old hook-hand out of hiding. Like, maybe we could make it a nice meal or something?"

"Would you do it for a Scooby Snack?" Velma offered.

Scooby and Shaggy glanced at each other. Shaggy's belly grumbled in response.

"Rokay!" Scooby said happily.

Captain Johnny showed Velma exactly how to find the treasure chest he'd hidden. Then Scooby,

Shaggy, Velma, and Fred set off into the woods to try to trick the pirate ghost into appearing again. The *Ruby Princess*'s crew and passengers, including Kurt, Barb, and Captain Johnny, remained behind on the beach.

Fred and Velma walked through the woods so briskly that Scooby and Shaggy practically had to run to keep up. After about ten minutes, Velma stopped suddenly.

"We'll set the trap and hide right here," she said. She dug under some furry-looking ferns and handed Shaggy the captain's treasure chest.

Meanwhile, Fred began to work on tying knots around the trees, creating a foolproof rope trap. "You guys go on up ahead. When you're in place, start shouting. As the pirate runs by, we'll snap it up in our trap and catch this crook once and for all!"

Scooby and Shaggy reluctantly walked a little farther into the woods. Scooby was carrying Captain Johnny's treasure chest on his back. He huffed and puffed as they trooped along.

It was only a few minutes before Shaggy found the rock that Velma had directed them to, the one shaped like a heart. It was in the middle of a nearby clearing, with a view of the sunny sky above them.

"Like, I just hope Fred's plan works," Shaggy

said. He opened Captain Johnny's treasure chest to peek at the fake gold and jewels inside.

"Re, roo," Scooby said. "Ri riss Raphne."

"Like, some of this stuff is pretty nice, Scoob," Shaggy said, poking his hands down to the bottom of the treasure chest. "Would you like a little pirate's booty for our mission?"

Scooby nodded, and Shaggy draped a thick gold necklace over his pal's neck. Shaggy placed a crown on his own head. They both began to giggle.

"Okay, Scoob, are you ready?" Shaggy asked.

Scooby nodded. They began to yell.

"We found it!" Shaggy shouted at the top of his lungs. "We found the pirate treasure! Not Captain Johnny's treasure, the *real* pirate treasure. Yoo-hoo! Everyone! It's back here!"

"Rold!" Scooby howled. "Rewels!"

"Like, we're rich!" Shaggy screamed.

The two friends could hear branches cracking and breaking as someone charged through the forest toward them. Scooby tucked his head under Shaggy's arm and shook with fear.

Would Fred's plan work? Would the rope trap catch the pirate ghost, or were Scooby and Shaggy next in line to be taken prisoner?

The footsteps came closer and closer. Scooby and Shaggy stopped yelling, hoping they'd be able to hear the sounds of Fred and Velma celebrating their catch.

Just then, something swung down from a branch on the other side of the clearing. It was the pirate ghost! It had come from the other way—it hadn't even gone past Fred's trap!

"Rhost!" Scooby cried, covering his eyes so he wouldn't have to look. "Raggy, ret's run!"

Shaggy grabbed Scooby's paw. They began to back out of the clearing and into the forest, heading in the direction of Fred and Velma's trap.

There was still a chance to catch the ghost. If they led it in the direction of Fred's trap, they could save the day.

Scooby and Shaggy edged closer and closer to Fred's trap. But the pirate ghost swung through the trees and dropped down on the ground between the two buddies and the rope trap! It laughed menacingly as it reached for them.

"Like, the treasure's all yours. Just leave me and Scooby alone," Shaggy said, his voice shaking.

The pirate cackled and drew closer. Shaggy and Scooby both turned to run the other way—but Scooby was just a moment too late. The pirate ghost reached out and hooked it's hand onto the golden necklace around Scooby's neck.

Scooby was trapped! He dug his feet into the ground and tugged at the necklace, trying to free himself from the pirate's hook. But the pirate tugged harder.

Scooby pulled again, but the villain leaned back and tugged with all its might, trying to drag Scooby away.

Scooby slipped the necklace off his neck. That did it! The pirate ghost stumbled backward. Those few steps were all it took. It was snared in Fred's trap!

Velma and Fred whooped and cheered. They had caught the ghost! It was hanging upside down from a big tree.

"Now let's see who's hiding under here," Velma said, pulling the mask off the pirate's face.

When he saw who it was, Shaggy gasped. "Like, what about my cheese biscuits?!"

CHAPTER 9

"*Arr!*" Purple Beard yelled. He waved his hook in the air and growled at the gang, who were safe and sound below him. "Get me down from here!"

Captain Johnny came charging through the

trees. "Purple Beard? Is it true? Did ya really take one of me passengers prisoner?"

"I did!" the ship's cook yelled. "And I'm not telling anyone where she is until you give me that treasure!"

"Like, there is no treasure," Shaggy said, laughing.

"No treasure?" Purple Beard growled. "I heard you say you found it. I want me treasure!"

"The real treasure is just a legend," Fred explained. "It's not real."

"Just like the ghost pirate isn't real," Velma added.

"Sorry, cook," Shaggy said. "Like, we tricked you." He turned to grin happily at Scooby, but Scooby was nowhere to be seen. "Scoob? Scooby-Doo, where are you?"

Scooby's bark rang out from off in the distance. "Raggy! Relma! Red!"

"What did you find, Scooby?" Velma asked, running through the trees.

"Rit's Raphne!" Scooby howled. "Rover rere!"

They left Purple Beard dangling in the tree and ran through the forest, following the sound of Scooby's bark. Their pal was standing at the base of a tree, chewing something. He pointed up.

Daphne was sitting in the crook of two branches, her hands and feet tied and her mouth covered with a piece of white shirt. *"Mmm, mmm, mmm!"* she cried through her gag.

"Daphne! Thank goodness you're okay," Fred cried. He, Velma, and Captain Johnny worked together to get her untied.

Shaggy turned to Scooby. "Like, Scoob? What are you eating? I don't think you're supposed to eat weird stuff you find in the jungle."

"Rit's randy," Scooby said happily.

"Where did you get candy?" Shaggy asked, looking around. "I want candy."

Daphne climbed down the tree to safety. "It's the candy I hid in my pocket this morning on the boat," she explained, patting Scooby on the back.

"I managed to pull it out of my pocket and throw it down to the ground, hoping one of you would see it. Scooby must have used his nose to find me. You saved the day, Scooby-Doo!"

Scooby beamed proudly. Fred and Velma gave Daphne a hand, and together they all walked back to the spot where they'd left Purple Beard.

"So I guess you figured out that Purple Beard is behind all this?" Daphne asked. She pointed to the unmasked pirate, who was still hanging from the tree.

Captain Johnny stared at his cook miserably. "I'm disappointed in ya."

Purple Beard glowered at him, but said nothing.

"How did you solve the mystery?" Daphne asked.

"Our first clue was the backpack we found in the woods," Velma said. "We found a *Ruby Princess* backpack on the ground in the very spot where you disappeared, Daphne."

Fred jumped in. "We realized that whoever took you prisoner must have dropped it. There were three people wearing a backpack just like the one we found earlier," he said. "Sassy Sally, Purple Beard, and Barb, Kurt's wife."

"Naturally, they seemed suspicious in other ways, too," Velma added. "But we were able to rule out Kurt and Barb as suspects pretty easily."

"That's right. You see, Kurt and Barb turned up right after Daphne disappeared," Fred chimed in, looking at Captain Johnny. "At first, that made them seem even more suspicious. But then we realized that it would have been really difficult to take Daphne prisoner, hide her somewhere, and get back to the place where she'd disappeared in just a few minutes."

Velma nodded. "That's right. *And* Barb was still wearing her backpack after Daphne disappeared—it got caught in a tree branch as they walked away from us. That's how we knew that they weren't involved." She turned to Purple Beard. "So that left us with two other suspects: Purple Beard and Sassy Sally."

Purple Beard growled. "How do you know it's not Sassy Sally that's responsible?"

"Well, for one thing," Velma said with a smile, "you're the one caught up in the tree right now. That makes you look awfully guilty."

"She's got a point," Captain Johnny said, nodding.

"We did think it was Sassy Sally for a while. The backpack was stuffed with hooks, which made us think Sally must be behind all of this," Velma added.

"But, Purple Beard, it was a bunch of knots that gave you away," Fred added.

Purple Beard furrowed his brow and scratched at his beard. "Knots? What are you talking about?"

"Well, the traps you'd placed out here in the woods to catch people were constructed using some very complicated ship knots," Fred said. "Nothing *I* couldn't figure out, but they're the sort of knots that we saw the deckhands using on the *Ruby Princess* today. One knot in particular—the Ruby Rope—is unique to the *Ruby Princess.* That's how we figured out it must have been one of Captain Johnny's deckhands behind all of this. The knots you used in your rope traps gave you away!"

"Arrrr!" Purple Beard growled.

Captain Johnny untied Purple Beard from the trap. When the deckhand fell to the ground, Captain Johnny quickly secured his arms behind his back and knotted them together again.

"But, Purple Beard, why did you do this?" Captain Johnny asked.

"I told you," Purple Beard said angrily. "I know there's buried treasure out here, and I want to be the one to find it! I would have, too, if it hadn't been for a bunch of meddling kids and their dog."

"You know, the story about real treasure and pirate ghosts is one *I* made up," Captain Johnny said, grinning. "I planted that story many, many years ago to make this whole cruise seem authentic. I've had the idea to run a pirate adventure cruise for years. If people thought there was a history of real pirates out in these parts, it would make people more interested in coming on me adventure."

Captain Johnny shrugged his shoulders. "I've been telling stories for years, hoping that someday when I got the *Ruby Princess* fixed up and out to sea again, I'd have people dreaming of pirate adventures—the chance to stumble upon some real treasure and explore old pirate stomping grounds."

"*You* started the legend of pirate ghosts and hidden treasure?" Purple Beard moaned. "So, it really is just a story? There's no real treasure?"

"All made up. There have never been real pirates around these parts," Captain Johnny said, grinning. "I guess I wove a good tale, since you all seemed to believe it. I just didn't think the promise of forgotten treasure would make anyone do something as crazy as what you've done, Purple Beard."

Purple Beard groaned and hung his head.

Shaggy gulped. "Like, guys? There's one important question left."

"What's that, Shaggy?" Daphne asked.

Shaggy grinned sheepishly. "Without Purple Beard in the kitchen, who's going to cook the pirate feast tonight?"

Captain Johnny smiled. "I know someone who's been hoping to get into the kitchen on the *Ruby Princess* fer quite some time," he said. "Sassy Sally can whip up a tasty fish fry, and I know she'd be happy to take over for Purple Beard."

"No!" Purple Beard cried. "That's my kitchen!"

"Not anymore, it's not," Captain Johnny said. "Yer gonna eat your supper below deck. That is, *if* Sally decides you deserve any dinner. But I don't think ol' Sally's going to be too happy with you after she hears what you've done." The captain laughed a big belly laugh. "And as for you kids . . . well, of course you're sitting with me at the Captain's Table. We'll be eating like pirates tonight, me hearties! You solved the mystery and saved the day."

"Rahoy!" Scooby-Doo barked, and everyone laughed. "Scooby-Dooby-Doo!"